A Manual of
HOUSE MONSTERS

A Manual of
HOUSE MONSTERS

STANISLAV MARIJANOVIC

To my daughters — s.m.

Published in the United States of America in 1999
by MONDO Publishing

For information contact:
MONDO Publishing, One Plaza Road, Greenvale, New York 11548
MONDO is a registered trademark of Mondo Publishing
Visit our web site at http://www.mondopub.com

Text adaptation by Howard Goldsmith
Design by Mina Greenstein
Production by The Kids at Our House
Printed in Italy by Grafiche AZ, Verona
First Mondo Printing, May 1999

99 00 01 02 03 04 05 06   HC   9 8 7 6 5 4 3 2 1
99 00 01 02 03 04 05 06   PB   9 8 7 6 5 4 3 2 1

Library of Congress Cataloging-in-Publication Data
Marijanovic, Stanislav, 1935-
A manual of house monsters / Stanislav Marijanovic.
    p.   cm.
Summary: Presents descriptions of monsters that cause all sorts of bad behavior.
ISBN 1-57255-718-4 (hardcover : alk. paper). — ISBN 1-57255-717-6 (pbk. : alk. paper)
[1. Monsters Fiction. 2. Behavior Fiction.] I. Title.
PZ7.M33847Man   1999
[E]—DC21   99-20138
                                                        CIP
                                                        AC

Introduction

House monsters are creatures that live in your home. They are not guests. They were not invited to live there. But they move right in anyway and cause all sorts of trouble.

House monsters are always planning mischief. They tug at you and trip you up. They make you do strange things. They make your life more difficult than you would like.

A Manual of House Monsters introduces the most common household monsters. These monsters are found in almost every home. They like to hide, so you may have to search for them. This manual tells you how to spot them all.

If you don't find any house monsters, don't worry. They will surely find you!

AHCHOO

the monster of sneezing

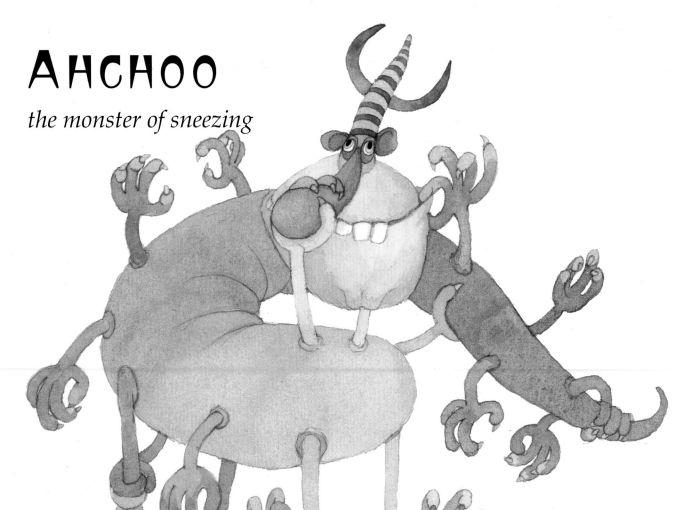

AHCHOO likes to curl up in snug, warm places for the winter. As soon as the weather starts to turn cold, Ahchoo begins his search for a winter home. Once he moves in, he seldom moves out before spring. He sniffles and sneezes giant, ear-splitting sneezes. Soon everyone nearby catches the sniffles. Choruses of *Ahchoo! Ahchoo! Ahchoo!* are heard everywhere. If you don't want a red, runny nose this winter, carry a pack of tissues and run when you see Ahchoo.

REFLECTUS

the mirror monster

REFLECTUS hides behind the mirrors in bathrooms and bedrooms. The moment you see your reflection, Reflectus holds you in her spell. She delights you with her songs as you stare at yourself for hours. *How cool I am*, you think. Reflectus also keeps you stuck in front of the bathroom mirror when Dad is in a hurry to finish shaving or your sister is waiting to wash her hair. So the next time you pass a mirror, don't stop and stare. Reflectus may be hiding there.

FIDGETS

the monster of impatience

When FIDGETS attacks, you lose your patience completely. You pace up and down. You grumble and whine. You just cannot sit still. But when properly trained, this monster can actually help you. You learn to enjoy the excitement of being impatient—for your birthday to come, for snow to fall, for summer vacation to start. Just don't let Fidgets give you the fidgets.

ALLMINUS

the monster of selfishness

Be on your guard against the sly ALLMINUS. She attacks unexpectedly with her familiar cries of "It's mine, all mine," and "I don't want to share." Some people say only children fight over things such as toys and candy. But Allminus attacks grown-ups just as much. Say "no" to selfish Allminus. It's much more fun to share.

CHATTERBUG

the telephone monster

CHATTERBUG moves into your home as soon as the telephone is installed. He cleverly hides inside the receiver. He feeds and grows on thick, juicy bits of conversation. Hot, cold, salty, or sweet—any conversation will do. Every time you use the phone you end up spending hours feeding him. Unfortunately, the phone company doesn't warn you about Chatterbug. You may not realize he is there until your mom receives the phone bill.

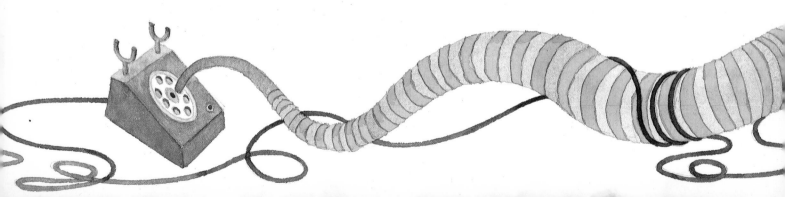

STUMBLETUMBLE

the tripping monster

STUMBLETUMBLE loves to watch a good stumble, tumble, or fall.
He hides under rugs, chairs, tables, and stairs, waiting to trip you. He
will chase the dog under the ladder when you climb up to the attic.
And he'll untie your shoelaces as you run to tell your brother to put
away his skates. Ooops! Too late. There goes Dad taking a slide.

OHNO

the monster of surprises

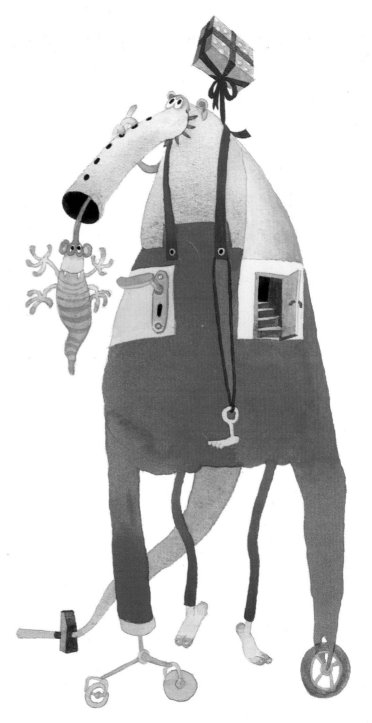

The thing OHNO likes best is a good surprise, usually at your expense. When no one is around, Ohno will get you to flood the bathroom. And if the walls in your home are painted white, they won't be for long. Not after your baby sister splashes orange juice, scrambled eggs, and ketchup on them. Not after she draws pictures on them. Who do you suppose gives your sister such ideas? Don't be surprised if it's Ohno.

DR. MISPLACE

the take-away monster

DR. MISPLACE is very nice, but troublesome. She follows you from room to room, snatching up things and tossing them where you seldom look. She takes away your pens and pencils, single socks, toys, and even the last piece of a jigsaw puzzle. She collects coins, keys, important notes, and electronic gadgets like remote controls. So be extra careful about where you put things, or Dr. Misplace will grab them.

TANTRUMELLA

the monster of yelling

TANTRUMELLA is the monster that makes you scream and shout, jump up and down, and yell at anyone who tries to talk to you. Sometimes you do this for no good reason at all. That's when adults will say you're having a tantrum. When you feel a tantrum coming on, take three deep breaths and count to ten. Then run if you see Tantrumella is still lurking around.

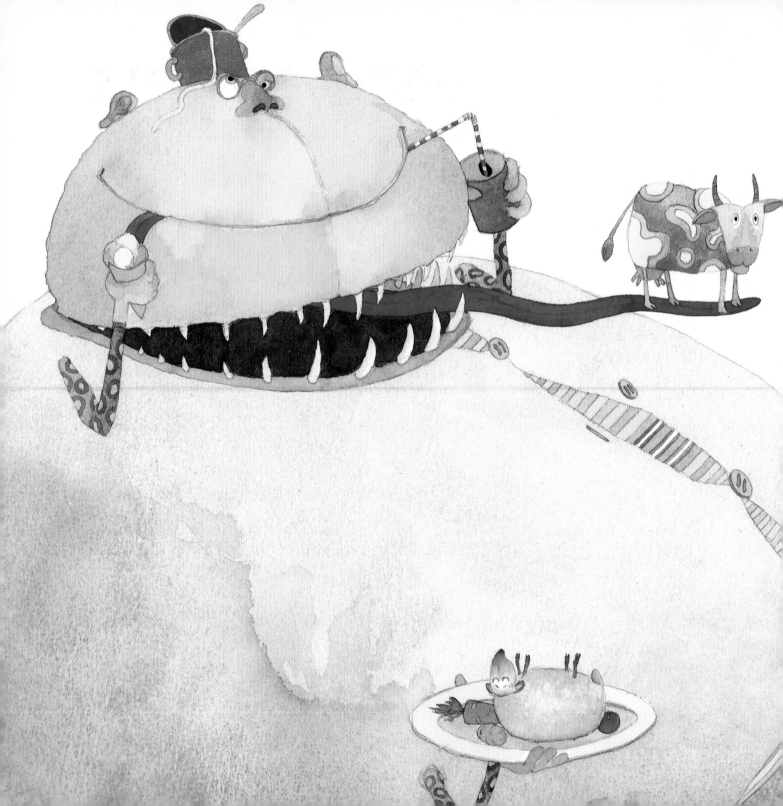

GOBBLEGOBBLE

the snacking monster

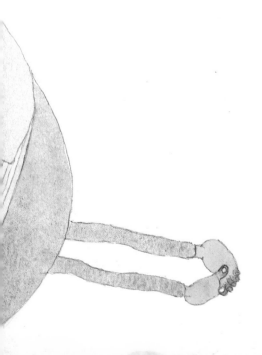

GOBBLEGOBBLE hides in the kitchen, particularly in the refrigerator and other places where food is kept. He strikes at almost any time, making you ready to snack. It could be in the morning, right after a meal, between meals, or even in the middle of the night. When Gobblegobble really gets naughty, he might make you munch on everything in sight—chips, ice cream, popcorn, cookies, pickles, meat loaf. This will surely spoil your appetite for your next meal.

SIZZLE

the monster of burns

SIZZLE is a very dangerous monster. She lurks behind the stove, under hot bowls and cups, and near other hot places. The sight of burned fingers or toes makes her glow with pleasure. She pushes your fingers toward the oven door and makes you lean against hot radiators. So the next time you're near something hot, stay alert, and watch out for Sizzle.

OOPSALO

the monster of spills

OOPSALO will do anything to cause a spill. He usually hides in the kitchen and bathroom. He makes you knock over the new bottle of shampoo, hold a mug full of cocoa with one finger, stir your soup too fast, or look away while pouring a glass of juice. Sponges, washing machines, and detergent make it easy to clean up, but Oopsalo is still a big nuisance to have around.

TOSS N. TURN and WORRYWART

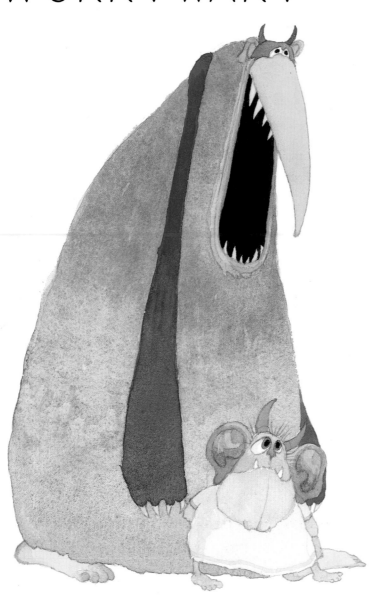

the keep-you-awake monsters

TOSS N. TURN and WORRYWART strike the moment you lie down to go to sleep. They fill your head with thoughts and ideas. *Where did I put my homework?* you ask yourself. *Am I still hungry? Did I feed the cat? Do I need to go to the bathroom again?* After worrying for a while, you call your mom to get some answers.

Try to avoid these monsters or you will never sleep a wink. If you think they are near, hum a tune, close your eyes, and stretch your arms and legs. Soon you'll be sound asleep.

SILLIUS

the monster of silliness

SILLIUS takes over when you are feeling bored. Suddenly you start doing silly things like trying to hang your clothes from the ceiling of your room. Then you might start bouncing a basketball on the kitchen floor. When this happens, stop and get some fresh air. Sillius hates fresh air, so ask someone to take you to the park immediately.

SHADOWY

the monster of the dark

SHADOWY comes out when you turn off the lights. She swirls and whirls through the dark, making everything in the room terribly frightening and scary. If you listen carefully, you will hear her singing, "A haunting we will go, a haunting we will go, . . ." But Shadowy is really a harmless old monster. If you switch on the light, she runs and hides. So just say, "Good night, Shadowy," and quietly go to sleep.

Turn this page at your own risk.

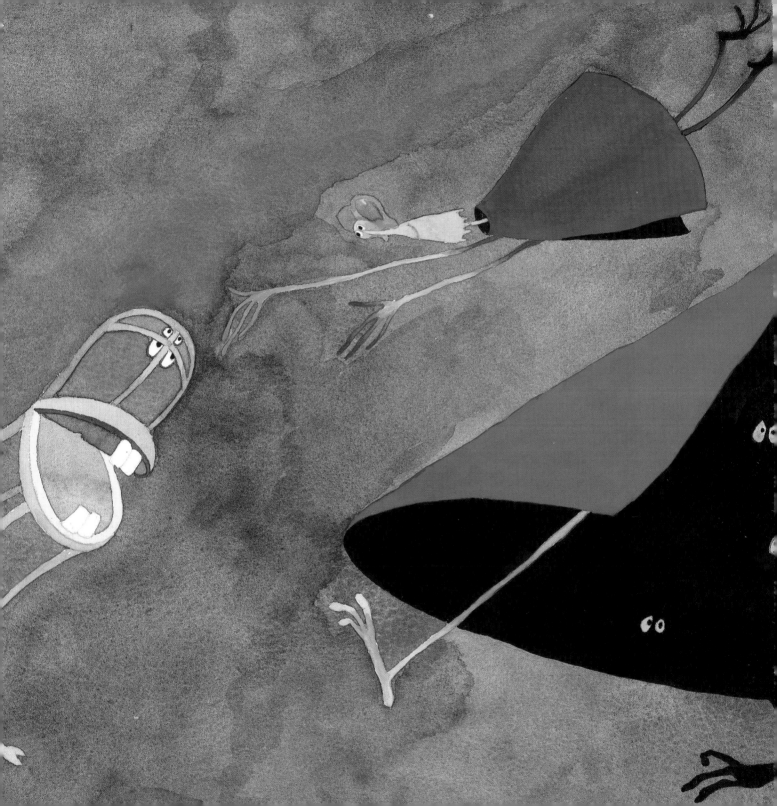

TEEVEE

the television monster

     TEEVEE looks harmless enough, resting between the sofa cushions or on a chair. But the moment you sit down he hands you the TV remote control. He forces you to turn on the television and sit there, eyes glued to the screen. He keeps you there for hours, watching show after show after show. You forget about everything else. You're stuck! The best defense against this monster is the simplest one. Turn off the television as soon as your favorite show is over.

THISORTHAT

the clothing monster

THISORTHAT strikes in the morning, especially before school. You stare at your clothes and wonder, *Should I wear this or that?* Whatever you put on first looks wrong. Your shirt looks too red, your pants look too blue, and your socks don't match anything. Thisorthat keeps handing you other clothes to try on and does not stop until everything is piled on the bed. The only remedy is to pick out what you will wear the night before.

NOWINKS

the monster of tiredness

You feel grouchy and cranky. You yawn and drag your feet.
You can hardly keep your eyes open. This can mean only one
thing—NOWINKS has struck. Nowinks is a clever monster
who works her mischief at night. She keeps you up well past
your bedtime playing video games, watching television, or just
fooling around. The next day you feel tired from head to foot.
So when Nowinks strikes, there is only one thing to do. Go
straight to bed and sleep, sleep, sleep. You will wake up feeling
happy and fresh. And that's a good thing, because tomorrow
is sure to be full of new house monster adventures.

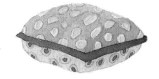